Berry Fairy Tales

Sleeping Beauty

By Eva Mason

Illustrated by Tonja & John Huxtable

Grosset & Dunlap

GROSSET & DUNLAP
Published by the Penguin Group
Penguin Group (USA) Inc., 375 Hudson Street, New York, New York 10014, U.S.A.
Penguin Group (Canada), 90 Eglinton Avenue East, Suite 700, Toronto, Ontario, Canada M4P 2Y3
(a division of Pearson Penguin Canada Inc.)
Penguin Books Ltd, 80 Strand, London WC2R 0RL, England
Penguin Ireland, 25 St Stephen's Green, Dublin 2, Ireland
(a division of Penguin Books Ltd)
Penguin Group (Australia), 250 Camberwell Road, Camberwell, Victoria 3124, Australia
(a division of Pearson Australia Group Pty Ltd)
Penguin Books India Pvt Ltd, 11 Community Centre, Panchsheel Park, New Delhi - 110 017, India
Penguin Group (NZ), Cnr Airborne and Rosedale Roads, Albany, Auckland 1310, New Zealand
(a division of Pearson New Zealand Ltd)
Penguin Books (South Africa) (Pty) Ltd, 24 Sturdee Avenue, Rosebank, Johannesburg 2196, South Africa

Penguin Books Ltd, Registered Offices:
80 Strand, London WC2R 0RL, England

Library of Congress Cataloging-in-Publication Data

Mason, Eva.
Sleeping Beauty / by Eva Mason ; illustrated by Tonja and John Huxtable.
p. cm. — (Berry fairy tales)
"Strawberry Shortcake."
Summary: An adaptation of the traditional tale, featuring Strawberry Shortcake
and her friends as the various characters.
ISBN 0-448-44274-4
[1. Fairy tales.   2. Folklore.]   I. Huxtable, Tonja, ill.   II. Huxtable, Tonja, ill.   III. Title.   IV. Series.
PZ8.M4482Sl 2006
398.2—dc22
2005012726

Special Edition ISBN 0-448-44138-1   10 9 8 7 6 5 4 3 2 1

nce upon a time, Strawberry Shortcake joined her berry best friends for a picnic. After they had eaten, Strawberry sighed with happiness. "That was the best picnic ever!" she exclaimed.

"Oh, Strawberry, our picnic's not over yet!" Rainbow Sherbet said. "Blueberry's going to read us a story!"

"I brought my favorite book of fairy tales," added Blueberry Muffin.

Blueberry Muffin began reading a story about a princess called
Sleeping Beauty. Strawberry curled up on the picnic blanket to listen
and soon fell into a sweet, dream-filled sleep. In her dream there was a
place called the Berry Kingdom—a land filled with every kind of berry
imaginable. Strawberry could see the berries so clearly, it was almost
like she was really there . . .

"... Hear ye! Hear ye!" called the royal page. "Today we welcome our new berry princess, Strawberry Rose!"

The people of Berry Kingdom cheered as they gathered in the Royal Berry Garden to celebrate the birth of Princess Strawberry Rose. The enchanted berry fairies in the kingdom had also come to the party. They circled Princess Strawberry Rose's cradle to present their birthday gifts by the magic of their berry wands.

"Princess Strawberry Rose, I give you the gift of grace. May you never stumble or fall!" Gingerberry Fairy announced. She tapped her magic wand on the cradle with a shower of ginger dust.

"I give you the gift of wisdom. May you learn new things each day," said Rainbowberry Fairy. She drew a magic rainbow over the cradle with her wand.

"Princess, you're already as pretty as a ripe, red strawberry, but just to be sure, I give you the gift of beauty!" said Angelberry Fairy, sprinkling lilac sparkles over the baby.

"And I give you the gift of nurturing, so berries will grow big and sweet under your care!" exclaimed Orangeberry Fairy with a swirl of magic orange dust.

Then she turned to the youngest fairy, tiny Appleberry Fairy, who had just earned her wings. "Go on, sweetie," Orangeberry Fairy said to the little one. "Now you can give your gift to our lovely princess."

But before Appleberry Fairy could lift her wand, a dark cloud spread across the garden.

All at once, it became clear that someone was missing from the celebration. Out of all the berry fairies, there was one who had not been invited—Brambleberry Fairy. She lived so deep in a thicket of brambles that it was impossible for the royal page to deliver an invitation to her. Had she found out about the party, after all?

Suddenly, Brambleberry Fairy appeared in a swirl of smoke. "What about me?" she snapped angrily. "Can't I give our princess a gift?"

Before anyone could stop her, she cast her spell. "Strawberry Rose, my gift is this: On your most perfect day, when you least expect it, you will prick your finger upon the thorn of a brambleberry bush. And you will vanish forever!"

Everyone gasped in shock as Brambleberry Fairy disappeared. What could be done to save poor Strawberry Rose?

Then there was a flutter of tiny wings. Little Appleberry Fairy still had to give her gift to the princess. She couldn't undo the spell, but she could weaken its power. "Strawberry Rose won't vanish—just fall asleep!" she said. And so it was: If Strawberry Rose ever pricked her finger on a brambleberry bush, she would simply fall into a deep, peaceful sleep.

The fairies breathed a sigh of relief. No one could sleep forever.
Their darling princess would be spared!

Still, to be sure, the kingdom banned all brambleberry bushes from
the land. No untended berry patch could grow within sight of the castle.
It seemed as if Princess Strawberry Rose might avoid Brambleberry Fairy's
wicked curse, after all.

Strawberry Rose became the lovely girl everyone expected. She was beautiful, graceful, smart, and sweet—and she tended the Royal Berry Garden with the greatest of care.

On a very special day—Strawberry Rose's birthday—the princess went out to enjoy her garden. The sun sparkled in a bright blue sky, and the berries tasted sweeter than they ever had before.

Suddenly, Strawberry Rose noticed a berry patch that she didn't recognize. "A new kind of berry!" she exclaimed. "What a perfect gift for a perfect day!"

Strawberry Rose reached out to pluck a berry. But there were thorns in the way, and before she knew it, she'd pricked her finger! Poor Strawberry Rose! With that single prick from a thorn of the brambleberry bush, she became so berry tired. Before she could even yawn, Strawberry Rose fell into a deep, dreamless sleep.

Upon hearing the dreadful news, the berry fairies sped to the castle.
"What will the kingdom do without Strawberry Rose?" cried Orangeberry
Fairy. "Everyone will miss her, and strawberries won't grow without her!"
"Let's put all the people to sleep," suggested Rainbowberry Fairy. "That
will give us time to figure out how to reverse the spell."
The fairies used their magic to weave a spell of sleepiness over the castle.
Soon even the royal guard was fast asleep.

The fairies worked so fast that a little berry magic couldn't help but scatter about. This was how—by mistake—each fairy drifted off to dreamland with the rest of the Berry Kingdom.

Gingerberry Fairy had one last thought as the sleeping spell fell upon her: *Wait! With everyone asleep, who will end the sleeping spell?* Then her eyes closed as she, too, drifted off.

The castle was left unguarded; the only sounds in the kingdom were the snores and sighs of slumber. Without Strawberry Rose's care, the berry patch grew wild and untamed. Before long, the castle was buried in a tangled forest of thorns, vines, and leaves.

After many seasons, a traveling lad named Prince Huckleberry came by the tangle of berry vines that hid the castle. He recognized at once the spectacular strawberries that spilled out all over the ground. "I've heard tales of these berries! This must be Princess Strawberry Rose's castle. She needs my help!"

He took a deep breath and plunged into the forest of vines.

Prince Huckleberry followed the sound of snoring, braving the thorny brambles and dense bushes. He hadn't gone far when a twisting vine crept out of the thicket and wound around him.

"Stop! I won't let you get any closer!" called a voice from the shadows. It was Brambleberry Fairy! She'd used her magic to trap the prince.

"Please let me pass! I must find Strawberry Rose," Prince Huckleberry pleaded.

"No one invited me to the celebration when Strawberry Rose was born. Why should I let you wake her? She can sleep forever!" snarled Brambleberry Fairy.

"But how could anyone invite you to a party?" the prince said. "Even in my kingdom we know that the tangle of thorns around your cottage keeps anyone from reaching you."

Brambleberry Fairy was shocked. "I didn't realize . . . How could I have been so wrong?" The vines instantly released Prince Huckleberry.

"You're free to go," said Brambleberry Fairy sadly. "Now I'll return to my thicket where even the sun can't reach me."

"Wait!" Prince Huckleberry called. "We can help Strawberry Rose together."

Brambleberry Fairy hesitated. "I do want to set things right," she said. Suddenly, the thorns parted to reveal a path to the castle.

Prince Huckleberry and Brambleberry Fairy found Strawberry Rose asleep in her royal chambers. At her feet was her loyal servant, the royal guard, whose snores filled the room.

Prince Huckleberry wasn't sure how to wake Strawberry Rose. "Wake up!" he said, but she didn't stir. He tried jumping up and down, yelling in her ear, and tickling her with the feather from his cap—but nothing worked. "What should we do?" he said.

"I have to reverse the spell," said Brambleberry Fairy. As she closed her eyes, her wand started to shine. A cloud of deep violet sparkles swirled over Strawberry Rose. The brambleberry spelldust spread across the room, out the window, and all through the kingdom. In moments, every person in Berry Kingdom had woken up . . .

. . . Except for Strawberry Rose.

"She's still asleep!" cried Angelberry Fairy. "Something must be wrong!"

But the royal guard didn't hear her. He bounded across the bed and licked the princess's cheek. Strawberry Rose opened her eyes. The kiss had broken the spell!

And so, too, did Strawberry Shortcake open her eyes—to the kiss of her pet Pupcake. She sat up just in time to hear Blueberry Muffin read the very last line of the fairy tale: "And they all lived berry happily ever after!" Strawberry grinned. It was just how she hoped her dream would end!